The Boxcar Children® Mysteries

THE WINDY CITY MYSTERY

created by
GERTRUDE CHANDLER WARNER

Illustrated by Charles Tang

ALBERT WHITMAN & Company
Morton Grove, Illinois

Library of Congress Cataloging-in-Publication
Data is available from the Library of Congress.

ISBN 0-8075-5447-2 (hardcover)
ISBN 0-8075-5448-0 (paperback)

Cover art by David Cunningham.

J-M
c 3

Contents

CHAPTER 1

The Windy City

"Look for Chad," Grandfather Alden said.

He and the Alden children had just gotten off an airplane.

"We've never met Chad," Henry, who was fourteen, reminded him.

Grandfather smiled. "That's right," he said. "I forgot."

Twelve-year-old Jessie glanced around the airport. "What does he look like?"

"I haven't seen him in a long time,"

Grandfather answered. "I'm not sure I'd recognize him myself."

"There he is!" Benny said. He skipped toward a tall, thin young man.

The others followed.

"Welcome to Chicago," the young man said.

"Chad Piper!" Mr. Alden said. "You've grown up!" He introduced Chad to the Alden children.

Then Jessie said, "Benny, how did you know this was Chad?"

Chad held up a sign. It read ALDENS.

"I'm six!" Benny said. "I can read!"

"I wasn't sure I'd recognize you," Chad said, leading the group down the long hall. "So I made the sign."

Ten-year-old Violet thought it would be fun to spend the day just watching the people come and go. "This place is really big," she said.

"O'Hare is one of the largest and busiest airports in the world," Chad told her.

They picked up their luggage from the carousel and went to the parking garage.

When they were settled in the car and on their way, Chad asked the children, "Have you decided what you want to see?"

"They didn't have much time to plan," Mr. Alden said.

"Grandfather just told us about the trip two days ago," Henry added.

"No problem," Chad said. "I'm to be your guide when your grandfather and my father are busy."

Jacob Piper, Chad's father, owned Piper Paper Products. Mr. Alden, who owned a mill, had come to see him on business.

"We'll pick up some maps and brochures tomorrow," Chad continued. "Then you can decide what you want to see."

"Oh, look!" Violet exclaimed.

Ahead, the city skyline was golden in the late afternoon sun.

"There it is," Chad said. "The Windy City."

"Wow!" Benny said, pointing to a building that towered over all the others. "That building looks like a giant!"

"It's the Sears Tower," Chad told them.

"One hundred and ten stories high — counting the antennae on top. It's the tallest building in North America."

Before long, they turned off the expressway onto city streets. People hurried along the sidewalks and in and out of buildings.

Chad parked the car. "Here we are," he said.

Everyone got out. Henry helped Chad with the suitcases.

Benny tipped his head back to look up. This building was not one hundred and ten stories, but it was tall. "Is this where we're staying?" he asked.

Chad nodded. "Piper Paper Products owns an apartment here. My father keeps it for visitors."

Inside, a man in a blue uniform was talking on a phone.

Chad gave Mr. Alden a key. "Take the elevator to twenty," he said. "Apartment 2004. I'll be up in a few minutes."

As the Aldens entered the elevator, Violet glanced over her shoulder. "Chad's talking to the man in the uniform," she said.

Henry turned around to look. "That's the doorman."

Upstairs, Benny ran ahead, reading the numbers on the doors. "Here it is!" he said.

Mr. Alden unlocked the door and stepped back to let the children enter. The apartment had high ceilings and lots of woodwork.

On their right was a small kitchen. Benny went to the refrigerator. He opened it and peered inside. "Look at all this food!" he said. "Eggs and bacon and jam and milk and soda and . . . everything!" He closed the door. "I'm going to like it here."

Beyond the kitchen was a large living room. Violet crossed to the wall of windows.

Grandfather followed her. "There's Lake Michigan," he said.

A few blocks east, the lake sparkled.

"It's beautiful," Violet said.

Henry came up beside them. "It sure is," he agreed.

Jessie came into the room. "There are three big bedrooms," she told them.

"Grandfather can have one. Henry, you and Benny can have another, and Violet and I will take the third."

The other Aldens took their suitcases and followed her. Jessie was good at organizing things.

They were in their separate bedrooms when Chad came into the apartment and called, "Where is everyone?"

The Aldens returned to the living room.

"This is a nice place," Jessie said.

Chad grinned. "I'm glad you like it. I helped decorate it. It's a challenge — an old place like this."

"Are you a decorator?" Violet asked.

Chad shook his head. "Actually, I work part-time for my father," he said, "but I am going to school. I want to be an artist."

"Violet's an artist." There was pride in Benny's voice.

"Are you?" Chad said. "That's great!"

Violet blushed. "I'm not really an artist," she objected. "I just like to sketch."

"That's how I started," Chad told her. "I'd like to see your work."

"You brought your sketchbook, didn't you?" Henry asked.

Violet nodded. She always packed her sketchbook.

"Good," Chad said. "We'll make time to do some drawing." He turned to the others. "If everything's all right here, I'll let you get settled."

"Are we going to meet your father?" Henry asked.

Chad frowned. "I don't know. He's always busy with some new plan for his business. Thank goodness he has his hobby or he would never relax!"

Jessie wanted to ask what his father's hobby was, but Mr. Alden said, "I know you're busy. You run along. Tell your father I'll see him in the morning."

"And I'll be back bright and early to show you the city," Chad said to the children. He started out. At the door, he said, "Are there any questions about the apartment or anything?"

"I have a question," Benny piped up. "Can we eat anything we find?"

Chad laughed. "Anything," he said. "Just don't eat it all at once."

After Chad left, the Aldens unpacked.

When they had finished, Jessie said, "I have a surprise." She showed them a book about Chicago.

Grandfather Alden was more surprised than anyone. "That's my old school workbook. Where did you find it, Jessie?"

"In the bookcase at home," she answered.

"You used that book in *school*?" Benny said. He thought it must be very old, but he didn't say so.

"We were studying American cities," Grandfather said. He took the book from Jessie and glanced through it. "Soon after we finished our study, your great-grandfather brought me here on the train. Very few people traveled by airplane then."

"A train is still the best way to travel," Henry said, thinking of the boxcar he and his brother and sisters had lived in after their parents had died. When their grandfather found them, he brought the children and their boxcar to his home.

The others agreed with Henry. "You see so much more," Jessie concluded.

Grandfather closed the book. "This is a very old book," he said. "You will find things have changed."

The children sat down to study the book.

"Chicago's a terrific city," Mr. Alden put in. "It was a good city before the fire and a great one after."

"Fire?" Violet repeated.

Henry held up the workbook. "It tells about it in here," he told his sister. "It's called the Great Chicago Fire. It nearly destroyed the whole city way back in 1871." He showed the other Aldens a picture of a building. "That's the Water Tower — one of the few buildings that wasn't burned."

"How did the fire start?" Violet asked.

Henry studied the book. Then he said, "No one knows."

"The most popular explanation concerns a cow and a lantern," Grandfather said.

"That story is here in the book," Henry said. "People thought Mrs. O'Leary's cow kicked over a lantern and started the fire. High winds spread it."

"Is that why they call it the Windy City?" Benny asked. "Because of the winds?"

"Could be," Grandfather answered. "But most say it's because residents bragged so much about their city. People said they were windy — full of hot air."

Jessie said, "This city is full of mysteries!"

Grandfather agreed. "Those mysteries will never be solved," he said. "But here's one you can solve: Shall we eat supper here or go out?"

"Here!" the younger Aldens all said.

Grandfather started for the kitchen. "I'll be the cook tonight."

The children looked at one another. Grandfather seldom did the cooking.

"Do you want some help?" Jessie asked.

"You can set the table," Grandfather answered.

They decided to move the table nearer to the windows. Then Jessie and Violet poked through drawers until they found a table-cloth and silverware. Henry and Benny found the dishes.

"Oh, look," Benny said. "A pink mug!" It reminded him of the cracked pink cup he had used when they lived in the boxcar. "That'll be my cup," he said.

Before long, Grandfather announced, "Dinner's ready."

He brought five omelettes to the table.

"They look delicious," Violet said.

Benny took a taste. "Ummm. It *is* delicious!"

"You didn't know your old grandfather was such a good cook, did you?"

"All the Aldens are good cooks," Henry said.

"But how did you do it so fast?" Jessie asked.

"Ahh," Mr. Alden answered. "There's a mystery for you."

Benny poured milk into the pink mug. "That's our mystery for this trip," he said. "There won't be any more."

Grandfather tilted his head to one side. His eyes twinkled. "Don't be too sure of that, Benny. You children seem to attract mysteries."

CHAPTER 2

A New Mystery

Henry was the first one up in the morning. He made bacon and eggs and poured orange juice.

Benny came into the kitchen rubbing his eyes. "I smell bacon," he said.

Soon the others were up, too. Violet made toast. Jessie made coffee for Grandfather.

When he joined them in the living room, Mr. Alden said, "That's what I like to see: teamwork."

They sat before the large windows where

they watched the early sun trace golden paths across the lake.

"I wonder what we'll do today," Jessie said.

"Just be sure to wear comfortable shoes," Grandfather told them. "I'm sure you'll do a lot of walking."

The telephone rang. "Chad will be late," Grandfather said as he hung up.

"That's all right, Grandfather," Jessie said. "We aren't ready anyway."

Mr. Alden looked at his watch. "I have a meeting at Piper's office. I don't like to keep everyone waiting."

"You can go, Grandfather," Henry said. "We'll be fine."

"I'm sure you will be," Mr. Alden said. "I sometimes forget how responsible you are." He looked at his watch again. "Chad said he'd meet you downstairs in the lobby. We'll go downstairs together."

"Hurry up and get ready," Jessie directed. "We'll do the dishes later."

They were dressed and ready in a flash.

In the elevator, Mr. Alden gave Henry

the apartment key. "In case you get back before I do," he explained. "I'm sure Cob has
another key. I'll get one from him."

"Who's Cob?" Benny asked.

"Mr. Piper. His real name is *Jacob*, but
everyone calls him *Cob*."

"Cob Piper," Benny said. He liked the
sound of it.

Downstairs, the doorman was talking to
someone — a balding man with a bushy
mustache. Wearing bib overalls and carrying
a striped cap, he looked out of place. When
he saw the Aldens, he hurried away. The
doorman followed him out of the building.

Grandfather looked at his watch. "I have
to go," he said. "Are you sure you'll be all
right?"

"Of course, Grandfather," Henry said.
"We'll be fine."

"Well, then, I'll be on my way," Mr.
Alden said. "Have fun, and don't wander off
without Chad. This is a big city."

The Aldens sat down on a marble bench.

"Did Grandfather seem like he was act-
ing a little strange to you?" Jessie asked.

Henry nodded.

"He was probably just afraid he was going to be late for his meeting," Violet said.

Henry nodded. "Grandfather likes to be on time."

They fell silent, watching the people hurrying through the lobby. Outside, the doorman smiled at everyone who passed through the doors.

After a while Violet said, "I wonder where all these people are going."

"Most of them are probably headed to work," Henry said.

"What about that man with the big mustache?" Benny asked.

"He was dressed in overalls," Violet said. "I'll bet he doesn't work in an office."

"The city is full of all kinds of jobs," Jessie said.

"He looked like a railroad engineer," Henry added.

Just then they saw Chad outside. He stopped to talk to the doorman.

"Let's go." Henry stood up and started for the door.

"He's going away!" Benny observed as Chad hurried out of sight.

The doorman came in. "You must be the Aldens," he said, smiling. "I'm Willard. I have a message for you."

"From Chad?" Henry asked.

Willard nodded. "He says he'll be with you shortly. He had an errand down the street." He started away. "Oh, I almost forgot," he said, turning back. "This is for you, too." He handed Henry an envelope and went back outside.

"Who's that from?" Benny asked.

Henry studied the envelope. "It doesn't say."

"It's probably from Chad," Violet decided.

Henry opened the envelope and took out a piece of paper. "This is odd," he said, and he began to read the note aloud.

In this city
There's lots to do.
Follow my lead
To each new clue.

And when you've seen
All the rest,
You'll find the treasure
That is best.
NOTE WELL: DON'T TELL!

"Don't tell *what*, Henry?" Benny asked.

Henry shrugged. "I don't know. About the note, maybe, or . . . There's a clue on the bottom. Maybe that's it."

"A clue? What kind of clue?" Jessie said. Henry read on:

CLUE #1
Find a structure
Straight and tall
Standing there
Through fire and all.

They drifted back to the bench and sat down. They were full of questions. *What did this note mean? Who had written it? Why was it given to them? What was the special treasure the note mentioned?*

"Chad wrote the note," Jessie decided.

"But why?" Henry wondered.

"Let's ask him," Benny said.

"The note says, 'Don't tell,'" Violet reminded him.

Benny was puzzled. "But if Chad wrote it, he already knows about it."

"You're right, Benny," Henry said, "but if he *did* write it, he doesn't want us to know he did."

"It's some kind of game — a treasure hunt," Jessie said. "We should just go along with it."

"Then we'd better figure out the clue," Henry concluded. He reread it.

"A *structure* — is that a *building*?" Benny asked.

Henry nodded. "It could be a building. But there are other kinds of structures."

"Let's say it's a building, Henry," Jessie suggested.

"Okay. A building — straight and tall —"

"There's Chad!" Benny said.

This time Chad came inside. "Sorry I'm late," he said. "I hope you weren't bored."

Henry stuffed the note into his pocket.

"Actually, we were busy . . . figuring things out," he said.

The Aldens all watched Chad. If he had written the note, he would know they had been trying to figure out the clue. His reaction would give him away.

Chad did not react. Instead, he said, "Let's get moving!" and sailed through the doors with the Aldens at his heels.

Chad led the way along the broad sidewalks. "I hope you like to walk," he said.

Benny looked at the tall buildings and the busy streets. "Where are we going?" he asked.

"To the Water Tower," Chad answered. "It's not far."

"What's at the Water Tower?" Violet asked.

"Long ago it contained instruments to measure water pumped from Lake Michigan. Now it's a visitors' center," Chad said. "We can get information and maps there."

"The Water Tower!" Benny said. "We saw a picture of it in Grandfather's workbook. It looks like a castle."

"That's the one," Chad said.

Henry remembered something else about the building. He caught Jessie's eye. They dropped back behind Chad.

"What is it, Henry?" Jessie asked.

"The Water Tower — it survived the fire!" he whispered.

Jessie nodded. " 'A structure/ Straight and tall.' "

" 'Standing there/ Through fire and all,' " Henry completed.

Was the Water Tower the answer to the riddle?

"It can't be the place," Jessie decided.

"Why?" Henry asked. "It fits the clue."

"But if Chad wrote the clue, he wouldn't just take us there, would he?" Jessie said. "He'd want us to figure it out for ourselves."

That was true, Henry agreed. Why would Chad lead them to this place after he had gone to the trouble of writing the clue? He couldn't think of a single reason.

Finally he said, "Maybe he didn't write it."

"Then who did?"

"Jessie! Henry!" Benny called excitedly. "Hurry up!"

"We'll talk about this later," Henry said, and he and Jessie caught up to the others.

Just ahead, looking like some kind of fairy castle, was the Water Tower.

"No wonder it survived the fire," Henry said. "It's made of stone."

They went inside.

"Oh, look at the floor!" Violet exclaimed.

Blues, greens, purples, and yellows in flowing patterns glittered beneath their feet.

"Beautiful, isn't it?" Chad said.

"What's it made of?" Henry asked.

"Broken glass and stones and shells."

"I guess you can make art out of anything," Benny said.

Chad laughed. "If you know what you're doing."

They gathered information from the racks along the walls.

"Henry," Jessie whispered. "Look for another clue."

Henry didn't need to be told. He was already looking.

CHAPTER 3

No Clue

"That should be enough," Chad said. He led them outside and found a bench. "Let's sit here and look through the brochures."

Jessie and Violet studied the leaflets. Benny looked at the colorful pictures. But Henry couldn't concentrate. He kept wondering about the clue. He was sure they had come to the right place: The Water Tower was certainly the solution to the puzzle. But where was the next clue? He stared up at the stone building. What secret was it keeping? He stood up and walked toward it.

"Where're you going, Henry?" Benny asked.

"To look at the building close up," he said. He ran his hand along the rough stone walls and glanced down at the ground. Seeing something, he picked it up. But it was only a paper scrap. He went back inside the Water Tower.

"Did you find anything, Henry?" It was Jessie. She had come inside after him.

He shook his head. "If this is the place, there has to be another clue."

But there was nothing out of place — nothing there to get the Aldens' attention.

"Maybe we're wrong," Jessie continued. "Maybe this isn't the place."

Violet was at the door. "Grandfather's here!"

They went back outside. Sure enough, Grandfather Alden was sitting beside Benny on the bench.

"Grandfather!" Jessie said. "What are you doing here?"

"Cob and I finished our business for the

day," Mr. Alden answered, "so I thought I'd join you."

"How did you know we'd be here?" Henry asked.

"Well, I . . . uh . . ." Grandfather didn't seem to have an answer. Finally he said, "Chad told me. Didn't you, Chad?"

Chad looked confused. "Did I? I don't remember telling you."

"You did say we'd pick up brochures and maps this morning," Jessie reminded him.

"That's right," Grandfather said. "And this is a visitors' center — just the place to do that." Changing the subject, he asked, "What are your plans for the day?"

"We're still deciding," Violet said.

"I have a suggestion," Mr. Alden said. "How about a baseball game? The Cubs are in town."

Benny jumped up and down. "Oh, good!" he said. "We can have lunch there!"

Grandfather stood up. "Chad, we'd like you to come along."

"Thanks, I'd love to go, but I have some schoolwork to do," Chad said. He added,

"I'll see you in the morning," and then he was gone.

"Jessie, I think you dropped something," Grandfather said.

Jessie looked behind her. Several pamphlets lay on the ground.

"I'll get them," Benny said.

Mr. Alden picked up a few leaflets that had blown some distance away. He handed them to Jessie. "Don't forget these."

She stacked the papers and put them in her backpack.

"How are we getting to the ballpark, Grandfather?" Violet asked.

"You'll see," Mr. Alden answered. "Just follow me."

Benny laughed. "You made a rhyme, Grandfather! Just like the —" Henry poked him. Then Benny remembered they were not supposed to tell anyone about the mystery.

They walked west. Two blocks away, Mr. Alden led them down a broad staircase.

"We're going to the subway," Henry observed.

"There's a lot happening underground in Chicago," Grandfather said.

Downstairs, Grandfather Alden paid the woman in the ticket booth and, single file, they pushed through the metal turnstile. More stairs took them to the station platform where tracks ran along both sides.

Grandfather said, "We want to go north."

Violet was the first to see the NORTH-BOUND sign.

Before long, a train screeched to a stop. Doors slid open. They all hopped on.

After several stops, the train began to climb. It emerged from the tunnel into the sun. Up, up went the tracks until they were high above the street. The train screeched past the buildings lining the way.

"What do you think of the El, Benny?" Grandfather asked.

"El?" Benny said.

Henry looked at Grandfather Alden. "Is that short for *elevated*?"

"Right you are, Henry," Mr. Alden answered.

Before long, a voice came over the public address system. "Wrigley Field, home of the Chicago Cubs!" it said.

The train squealed to a halt. The Aldens followed the crowd down the steep stairway.

"The game's going to be crowded," Benny decided.

And he was right. Still, there was plenty of room. They found good seats.

"Is anybody hungry?" Grandfather asked.

Benny raised his hand. "I am!"

Laughing, the others raised their hands, too.

"Give me your orders," Mr. Alden said. "Henry and I will go get lunch."

They all wanted hot dogs and peanuts.

"That's easy to remember," Henry said. He followed Grandfather out to the concession stands.

Jessie, Violet, and Benny watched the pregame action. All around them, people settled into seats, talking excitedly.

"Did you think more about the clue?" Violet asked Jessie.

"Henry and I thought the Water Tower was the place," Jessie answered.

"You're right," Violet said. "It fits the description."

Benny was surprised. "You mean we solved that clue, and I didn't even know it?"

"We're not sure we solved it," Jessie said.

Violet thought about that. Finally she asked, "If Chad wrote the clue, why didn't he let us figure it out?"

"But who else could have written it?" Benny asked.

"Henry and I asked both those questions, too," Jessie answered. "And another thing: There was no clue at the Water Tower. There has to be another clue. Where is it?"

Just then, Henry appeared, carrying a box of drinks. "Grandfather has the food," he said. He looked over his shoulder. Mr. Alden wasn't there. "That's funny. He was right behind me."

Benny got to his feet. "Let's go find him. I'm hungry." He and Henry trotted off.

"Where could he be?" asked Jessie.

"Look!" Violet said. "Up there!"

Jessie followed her sister's gaze.

High at the top of the bleachers, a man

wearing bib overalls and a cap took a seat.

"Isn't that the man we saw this morning?" Violet asked.

"It's hard to tell," Jessie answered.

"There's Grandfather!" Violet said. She stood up and waved.

"Where are Henry and Benny?" Grandfather asked as he approached.

"They went to look for you," Jessie told him.

Just then, the boys scampered down the stairs to join them.

"What happened to you, Grandfather?" Henry asked. "You were right behind me and then you . . . disappeared."

Grandfather handed the box of food to Jessie. "Sorry, I . . . uh . . . went back to get this." He pulled a cap out of his pocket and put it on Benny's head. It was blue. On the front was a red letter: C. "Now you're a real Cubs fan," he said.

Henry was puzzled. He had been with Grandfather when he bought the cap. Had Grandfather forgotten?

Benny passed out the food. "This smells so good," he said.

A voice boomed out over the field. "Plaaaaay ball!"

The teams took their positions.

The game began!

The crack of the bat, the shouts of the umpires, and the roar of the crowd soon pushed the mystery to the back of the Aldens' minds.

During the seventh inning, Grandfather Alden went for more peanuts. "Be right back," he said.

Watching him go, Violet saw someone else. "There's that man again," she said.

The man in the overalls hurried past. He was definitely the same man they had seen speaking with the doorman, yet he looked different somehow.

Benny giggled. "His mustache is crooked!" he said.

This time, Grandfather returned with the peanuts quickly. The Aldens enjoyed the rest of the game, and best of all, the Cubs won!

CHAPTER 4

Another Clue

Back at their apartment building, Willard opened the door for them. "How'd you like the ball game?" he asked. "When those Cubbies are good, they are really good."

Wide-eyed, Benny looked up at the man. "How'd you know we went to the game?"

Willard raised one eyebrow. "This is my building. I know all about the people in it."

The Aldens laughed — except Benny. He was wondering if Willard could be the man behind the mysterious clue.

Upstairs, Grandfather said, "I think I'll take a nap. All that rooting for the home team wore me out."

"You go ahead, Grandfather," Jessie said. "We'll do the breakfast dishes."

"If I'm not up, wake me in an hour," Mr. Alden said as he closed his bedroom door.

Violet helped with the dishes. "Next time, it's your turn," she said to her brothers.

After everything had been dried and put away, Jessie said, "We should decide where we want to go tomorrow with Chad." She took the brochures out of her backpack and laid them on the table.

Benny leaned in close to the others. "I think Willard wrote the clue," he whispered.

"Willard?" Henry said. "I doubt it."

Violet disagreed. "Benny might be right," she said. "Willard did give us the note, remember? And he never said it was from Chad."

"We didn't ask him," Henry said.

"That would explain why Chad took us to the Water Tower before we figured it out," Jessie said. "He didn't know about the clue."

"Willard did it," Benny said. "How else did he know we went to the ball game?"

Henry, Jessie, and Violet exchanged amused glances.

"Benny, you're the clue to that," Henry said.

Benny pointed to himself. "Me?"

Henry reached across the table and took the cap off Benny's head. "You're wearing a Cubs cap," he said.

Benny put the cap back on his head. "Oh, I forgot," he said.

Violet shuffled through the pamphlets. She held up a white envelope. "What's this?"

Jessie took it from her. "I don't know," she said. "There's no writing on it." Jessie opened it and took out a folded piece of paper. "It's another clue!" She read it aloud:

CLUE #2
When you hear
Two lions roar,
You are at
The proper door.
Go inside,
Walk around,
Find tiny rooms
On the ground.

Jessie looked up from the paper. "I must have gotten this at the Water Tower," she said.

"But I looked everywhere," Henry said. "There was nothing."

"You dropped some stuff, Jessie," Benny reminded her. "I picked it up. Maybe the clue was mixed in with that."

"Or it could have been with the things Grandfather picked up," Violet said.

Jessie reexamined the envelope. "But our name isn't on this," she said.

"Whoever put it there was sure we'd find it," Henry decided.

"Who knew we were going to be there?" Violet asked.

They could all answer that: Chad and Grandfather.

"Grandfather certainly didn't do it," Jessie said.

Henry nodded. "Chad's behind this."

"Or maybe Willard," Benny piped up. "He said he knows everything about the people in this building."

"We know one thing for sure," Violet said. "The Water Tower is definitely the answer to the first clue."

"How about this one?" Benny asked. "What's the answer to it?"

Jessie read the clue to them again. Then she sighed. "This one is really hard."

"Let's take it one line at a time," Henry suggested.

"The first is about lions roaring," Benny said.

"Zoos have lions," Violet put in.

"But do they have doors?" Jessie asked.

"Not the zoo itself," Henry said, "but the lion house would have doors."

"What about the little rooms?" Benny asked.

"*Tiny* rooms," Jessie corrected. "The clue says 'tiny rooms/ On the ground.' "

"Ants make tiny rooms," Benny said.

"Most of an anthill is *under* the ground," Henry said.

They heard Grandfather's voice in the bedroom. He was talking on the telephone.

Jessie piled the clue with the brochures and put them aside. "We'll get back to this later," she said.

Mr. Alden came into the room. "How about a picnic supper?"

Everyone thought that was a wonderful idea.

"Why don't you make sandwiches," he suggested. "I'll go downstairs to get a newspaper."

Jessie got out the bread, cold cuts, lettuce, and pickles. Benny got out the peanut butter and jelly. Violet took apples from the crisper and bananas from a bowl on the counter. Henry found paper plates and napkins.

"We can use my backpack to carry everything," Jessie said as she wrapped the last sandwich.

"Are there picnic tables where we're going?" Violet wondered aloud.

"We'll have to ask Grandfather," Henry said.

Benny went to the door and looked out into the hall. No Grandfather. "What's taking him so long?"

Mr. Alden *had* been gone a long time. Jessie wondered if something had happened to him. She did not want to alarm the others. "Let's look at the brochures while we wait," she said. "We haven't decided what we want to see tomorrow."

They had just sat down at the table when Grandfather came in.

"Where *were* you so long?" Benny asked.

Mr. Alden smiled. "I stopped to talk with Willard," he explained.

"We're ready to go," Violet told him.

"We'll need something to sit on." Grandfather looked around the apartment. In the hall closet, he found a blanket with a note taped to it. It said: FOR PICNICS.

"The Pipers thought of everything," Henry commented.

"Enjoy the concert," Willard said as they went out the door.

"We're going to a concert?" Violet asked. She loved music and played the violin.

"That we are," Mr. Alden answered.

"With a picnic supper?" Benny said. He couldn't imagine eating in a concert hall.

"This is a very special concert," Grandfather told him.

They walked along Michigan Avenue. Most of the shops and offices were closed now, but still the sidewalks were bustling with people.

Mr. Alden and Henry, who carried Jessie's backpack, were in the lead. Jessie, Violet, and Benny followed close behind. They approached a building fronted by a broad stairway.

"Look!" Benny said. "Lions!" He stopped abruptly.

Jessie and Violet stopped, too. They stared at the two large bronze lions on either side of the staircase. Each of the children was thinking the same thing: Could this building be the destination hinted at in Clue #2?

"We found it!" Benny said.

"But these lions don't roar," Jessie said.

"They *look* like they could," Benny answered.

Violet agreed. "They seem so real," she said. "I can almost hear them roar, too."

Thinking of the clue, Jessie said, "The place has doors."

"And an inside," Violet said.

"But what about the tiny rooms?" Benny asked.

Henry called to them.

"Coming!" Jessie responded. To Violet and Benny, she said, "We'll have to ask Chad about this building."

They followed Grandfather and Henry into Grant Park. Ahead were several rows of seats. Beyond those was a covered stage.

"A band shell," Violet said. "It's an outdoor concert!"

"It won't start for a while," Grandfather said. "We'll have our picnic while we wait."

They found a spot on the lawn and

spread out the blanket. Jessie began un-
packing her backpack.

Grandfather pointed to a concession
stand. "We can buy drinks here," he said.
"Come on, Violet."

When they had gone, Jessie asked Henry,
"Did you see those lions in front of that
building?"

Henry nodded. "What about them?"

"The clue!" Benny said.

Henry's eyes opened wide. "Oh," he said.
"I didn't think about that." He added, "But
those lions — they aren't real."

Benny laughed. He imagined those two
big greenish lions roaming the streets of
Chicago. "I'm glad they're not," he said. He
ran over to help carry the drinks.

Jessie handed the sandwiches around, and
everyone took an apple or a banana.

It was a beautiful evening. They ate their
supper and talked and joked. No thought of
the mystery entered their minds.

The concert started just before dark.
Benny lay back on the blanket. Before long,
he was asleep.

The other Aldens listened to the music. "The blues," Grandfather called it.

Overhead, the sky was clear and star-filled. Surrounded by the music and the twinkling lights, the Aldens felt as though they were in a magical city.

But eventually the concert ended, and they joined the streams of people reluctantly leaving the park.

Rubbing his eyes, Benny asked, "Are we going home now?"

"There's just one more stop," Grandfather said, and he led them to a large fountain.

"This is Buckingham Fountain," Grandfather said. "It's a real treasure."

The word *treasure* reminded them of the mystery. Each of the Alden children thought about the same words in the first note: "And when you've seen/ All the rest,/ You'll find the treasure/ That is best." Everything they had seen that day was interesting. Each was a treasure in its own way. How would they ever know when they had discovered the best?

CHAPTER 5

Two Lions and Tiny Rooms

Chad arrived the next morning just as they were finishing breakfast. After the children told him what they had done the day before, Chad asked, "And what do you want to do today?"

Jessie held up the brochures. "These should help us decide," she said.

Grandfather came into the living room. He said, "Good morning, Chad." Adding, "See you later. I have a meeting with Cob Piper," he went out the door.

Chad thumbed through the pamphlets.

"Museums, historic places, theaters — you name it."

"Is there a zoo?" Henry asked.

"The Lincoln Park Zoo isn't too far," Chad answered. "We could take a bus."

"Do they have lions?" Benny asked.

Chad nodded. "Last time I was there, there were two," he answered.

The Aldens exchanged glances. *Two* lions! The zoo could be the answer to the second clue.

"How about tiny rooms?" Benny asked.

Chad looked puzzled. "Tiny rooms?"

Violet put a finger to her lips. Benny understood. He had almost told Chad about the clue. Jessie changed the subject. "We passed a building last night on the way to the concert," she said. "There were lions in front of it."

Chad beamed. "The Art Institute. I go to school there."

"We'd like to go there," Henry said.

"Great!" Chad responded. "I was going to suggest it. I thought Violet might be interested."

"We're all interested," Jessie said.

Henry stood up. "Let's go," he urged.

Downstairs, Willard held the doors for them. "So the Aldens are off on another adventure," he said. As they walked away, he called, "I hope you find what you're looking for."

Jessie whispered, "Did you hear that?"

All of the Aldens had heard it. Willard must know they were looking for the answer to the clue. If not, why would he say anything about finding what they were looking for?

Chad, who was a few steps ahead, stopped and turned. "Hear what?" he asked.

"Oh, nothing," Benny said. This time he remembered not to say anything that would give them away.

Then Henry surprised him by saying, "Willard said he hopes we find what we're looking for. We wonder what he means." He watched Chad closely. If he and Willard were in this together, he might give himself away.

Chad shrugged. "He means what he says.

You *are* looking for something, aren't you?"

Amazed, the Aldens stared at him.

"People come to a new place for a reason," Chad said. "They're looking for something — to learn or to have fun or to find . . . something. When I go to a new place, I try to find an object or a person that would make a good painting. Whenever my father goes someplace, he looks for something about his hobby."

Again Jessie wondered what Mr. Piper's hobby might be, but suddenly Benny exclaimed, "Look at the bridge!"

Ahead, traffic was stopped. The Michigan Avenue Bridge was angling up into the air.

"How will we get around it?" Henry asked.

"We'll just wait," Chad said. "It'll go down soon."

He led them to the side of the bridge. Below them, boats with tall masts moved along.

Jessie saw something else. "What's down there?"

"Lots," Chad said. "You're looking at a

tour boat landing. But there's a lower level, under the main streets."

"You mean with roads and everything?" Benny asked.

Chad nodded. "In some places there are train tracks and stores and restaurants."

"Like a double-decker city," Henry said.

The bridge moved back into place. The gates lifted. Traffic once again streamed over the bridge.

Before long, they came to the bronze lions. Violet was the first up the long stairway and through the revolving doors. The others were close behind her.

Behind the polished wood information center, a marble stairway went up to the sunlit floor above.

"This place is big," Benny said. "Where do we go first?" He was wondering where they might find tiny rooms.

Chad led them downstairs. "I thought you might like to start on the lower level," he said. "We'll pick up a brochure. But I'll have to meet you later. I have work to do."

They agreed to meet later in the lobby.

"Or, if I finish quickly, I'll look for you," Chad said as he hurried off.

Henry studied the brochure. The Aldens wandered around the museum, stopping along the way to admire displays of armor, an Egyptian mummy case, and ancient jewelry. But there were no tiny rooms.

"Where are the tiny rooms?" Jessie asked.

"We're in the wrong place," Benny said. "We have to go to the zoo."

It was nearly time to meet Chad. The Aldens headed toward the lobby.

Henry hung back. He looked at the map again. "Wait a minute!" he said.

At the same moment, Jessie stopped short. "Look!" She pointed to a sign over a doorway.

Together, she and Henry said, "The Thorne Miniature Rooms."

Inside this gallery they found tiny room after tiny room. Each represented a different time and a different place. Each held furniture and articles of the period.

The children were fascinated. They lingered at one room after another.

Finally Violet said, "Two lions and tiny rooms! We've found it!"

"But the clue says 'tiny rooms/ On the ground,'" Jessie reminded them. "These rooms aren't on the ground."

"The cases they're in are on the floor," Benny said. "Maybe the clue writer meant to say *floor*."

Violet agreed. "*Floor* didn't rhyme, so he used *ground*."

Henry was deep in thought. Finally he said, "He meant *ground*, all right. This is the ground floor."

"We've found it!" they all said at once.

"So these are the tiny rooms you were asking about," Chad said as he came up beside them. "How did you know about them?" Before they could say a word, he answered his own question. "You read about them in the brochure."

"Right," Henry said, "we read about them." He didn't go on to say, *in the second clue*.

"I'm hungry," Benny said.

Chad laughed. "Me, too. This place always makes me hungry. Probably because there are so many beautiful paintings of food."

He took them to an outdoor courtyard. They found a table near the center fountain.

They were no sooner seated than Chad said, "Oh, I forgot. I was supposed to leave a message for a friend of mine." He took a square white envelope from his back pocket. "I told him it'd be on the student bulletin board." He stood up. "I'll be right back."

As he hurried away, Jessie said, "Do you suppose that's the next clue?"

"In Chad's envelope?" Violet asked.

Jessie nodded.

"Why would he tell us that story about leaving a note for his friend?" Henry said. "He could have just given us the envelope and said he found it somewhere."

"Maybe he knows we suspect him," Benny said. "He's trying to throw us off his trail."

Jessie spotted a man across the room. Although his back was to them, he looked familiar. His dark hair circled a bald spot.

Below his suit coat, he wore overalls. "There's that man again."

They all looked at him.

Remembering the man's mustache had been crooked when they saw him at the ball game, Benny giggled.

Just then the man turned around. He had *no* mustache! And very bushy eyebrows!

"No mustache," Violet observed. "He's not the same man."

"He could have shaved it," Henry suggested.

"And put it over his eyes," Benny joked.

The man turned on his heel and hurried away.

"He certainly looks like that other man," Jessie said. "Maybe they're brothers."

They talked about that possibility until Chad returned.

He looked strange — pale and dazed. "You're not going to believe this," he said. "I think someone's following us." He held up a white envelope. "I found this on the student bulletin board. It's addressed to you!"

CHAPTER 6

Picture, Picture

After a moment's stunned silence, Henry reached out for the envelope.

Chad handed it over. "Who would leave a message for you here?"

"That's what we'd like to know," Benny said.

Even though she knew this must be the third clue, Jessie said, "Maybe it's from Grandfather." She watched Chad closely.

Henry went along with the pretense. "That could be." He, too, watched Chad closely. The young man seemed genuinely surprised to find the note here. Was he faking? There was no way to tell. "Maybe Grandfather wants us to meet him later."

"But Grandfather didn't know we would be here," Benny said.

Chad sank into a chair. "He might know," he said. "I called my father's office when we got here."

"Did you talk to Grandfather?" Henry asked.

Chad shook his head. "He and my father had gone. I left a message."

Henry folded the envelope and put it in his pocket.

Chad frowned. "Aren't you going to open it?"

"We'll read it later," Henry said.

Benny was curious about the note. "But Henry," he protested, "if it's from Grandfather —"

Just then a waiter came to take their order.

After lunch, Chad said, "I thought we might go down to the lake. Violet and I could get in some sketching."

Violet's shoulders drooped. "Oh, I didn't bring my sketchbook," she said sadly.

Chad tapped his knapsack. "I have an extra."

He led them out of the building and around the corner. At the lake, boats bobbed beside narrow piers. Out beyond the harbor, sails moved along the horizon.

"This looks like a good place," Chad said. "Does anyone else want to give it a try? I have plenty of sketch paper."

"Jessie and I will take a walk," Henry said.

Benny sighed. "I'd like to do that, too."

Chad laughed. "I'll get Violet set up." He gave her a sketchbook and several pencils.

Violet studied the scene. "I'll never get the shadows right," she said.

"You will," Chad assured her. "I'll show you how."

Henry, Jessie, and Benny walked along the lake, checking every now and then to be sure Chad wasn't watching them.

Finally Henry opened the envelope.

"Is that the same envelope Chad had?" Benny asked. "The one he was going to put on the bulletin board for his friend?"

Henry shook his head. "That one was square. This one is a rectangle." Henry carefully unfolded it. "It says 'CLUE #3.'"

Benny hopped up and down impatiently. "Read the rhyme!"

This time it wasn't a rhyme. It was a picture made up of cut-out sections from other pictures.

"A collage," Jessie said.

It showed a cow, a lantern, and burned-out buildings. In the foreground was a picture of a modern fire engine.

"Oh, this one's easy." Benny pointed at the picture. "That's Mrs. O'Leary's cow and this is her lantern — the one the cow kicked over —"

"*Supposedly* kicked over," Jessie corrected him. "Remember, Benny, that's just one possible story."

Benny waved that away. "And all these buildings — that's how the city looked after the Great Chicago Fire."

Jessie studied the picture. "I think you're right, Benny."

"But what about the fire engine?" Henry said.

"That's supposed to be one of the trucks that tried to put the fire out."

"I don't think so, Benny," Henry said. "This is a modern fire engine."

"But why would he put a picture of a new fire truck with all that old stuff?" Benny asked.

Although it looked easy, this clue could prove to be the most difficult of all.

They headed back to join Violet and Chad. On the way, they saw Willard sitting on the cement wall. His shirtsleeves were rolled up and his eyes were closed. His jacket and hat lay beside him.

"What's he doing here?" Jessie whispered.

"Following us," Benny answered.

Henry approached the man. "Let's ask him."

Jessie hung back. "Maybe we shouldn't disturb him."

But Willard's eyes snapped open and he looked right at them. He smiled. "Well,

well," he said. "If it isn't the Aldens. Still looking? Or have you found it?"

Benny glanced at his sister and brother. His look said, *I told you so.* He had been right: Willard had something to do with the treasure hunt.

"Have we found what?" Henry asked.

Willard lifted his hands, palms up. "Whatever it is you're looking for."

Benny started to say, *I think you know what we're looking for.* Before he could get it out, Jessie interrupted.

"Do you come down to the lake often?" she asked.

"Every chance I get. Especially in weather like this."

Violet called to them.

"See you later, Willard," Henry said, and the three Aldens went off.

"He's the one," Benny said.

Jessie and Henry said nothing. Each was wondering if Benny could be right after all.

Violet came running toward them. "Look at this! Chad taught me how to hold my pencil to do the shading." She showed them a sketch of a boat moored to a pier.

"This is really good," Henry said.

Chad smiled. "Violet's very talented."

Violet blushed. She did not think she was an artist yet, but there was no doubt that she was on her way to becoming one.

They strolled back to the apartment. Willard was not there. Another doorman greeted them.

Upstairs, Henry couldn't find the key. "I forgot to take it with us this morning," he explained.

"Knock on the door, Henry," Jessie suggested. "Maybe Grandfather's inside."

No one answered.

"No problem," Chad told them. "I have a key." He dug a ring of keys out of his pocket, selected one, and opened the door. Then he looked at his watch.

"You don't have to stay," Henry told him.

"I do have some work to do," he said.

"Grandfather should be along soon," Jessie said.

Knowing they would be all right without him, Chad left.

Henry took the new clue out of his pocket. "Violet, take a look at this," he said.

As Violet studied the picture, Benny explained it.

"I don't think the new fire engine is a mistake," she said.

"Neither do Henry and I," Jessie said.

"But what can it mean?" Violet asked.

Before they had time to figure it out, Grandfather came in. "Is everybody ready for dinner?" he asked.

Henry slipped the clue in with the maps and leaflets.

"Is it dinnertime already?" Benny was surprised. He had been so engrossed in the clue that he had forgotten all about eating.

Mr. Alden laughed. "Don't tell me you're not hungry, Benny!"

"Oh, I am," Benny answered. "I just didn't know it."

Willard was back on duty, and he hailed a cab.

"Where're we going?" Violet asked as she slipped into the backseat.

"To a very special place," Mr. Alden said.

The cab stopped before a brick building with striped awnings. People sat at white tables in the small front yard.

"Let's eat inside," Grandfather said.

They found a table by a bay window.

Henry went over to a display case full of photographs and other souvenirs. "This is the birthplace of deep-dish pizza," he told them when he returned.

They ordered a large pizza with everything.

"*Numero uno,*" the waiter said. "A good choice. Number one."

It was, indeed, a good choice. They had never eaten a better pizza.

On the way out, Benny said, "They deserve all those plates."

They arrived back at the apartment tired and happy.

"I think I'll go to bed," Jessie said.

They all decided to do the same.

It wasn't long before they fell asleep.

Later, the telephone woke everyone except Benny.

Grandfather answered it. His voice was muffled. Still, they heard a part of the conversation.

"No, no," he kept saying. Other words and phrases drifted in to them less clearly. "Trouble?" he said, and, "I don't want that. You'll just have to wait."

"Violet?" Jessie whispered. "Did you hear that?"

But Violet had drifted back to sleep.

In the other room, Henry lay in the dark wondering what this was about. Grandfather sounded so . . . different. Was something wrong? Could he be in some kind of trouble?

CHAPTER 7

Old Stories and New Fire Engines

"Grandfather," Henry called softly. He tapped on Mr. Alden's bedroom door.

From the kitchen, Jessie said, "Tell him breakfast is ready."

Henry called again. He waited. No sound. He opened the door and took a few steps into the room. "Grandfather's not here," Henry told the others.

"He's probably downstairs getting the paper," Benny said.

Jessie sank to a chair. "I don't think so," she said. "He had a strange telephone call last night."

"I heard that call, too," Henry said.

Benny shot to his feet. "Let's go find him!" He started for the door.

"Benny, wait!" Jessie commanded. "The phone call might have been from Mr. Piper. Grandfather was probably talking to him about the paper business."

Benny wasn't convinced. "I still think we should look —"

A key turned in the lock. The door opened. Grandfather came in, carrying a newspaper.

Smiling broadly, he said, "It's a fine morning!"

Benny rushed at him, arms outstretched. Laughing, Grandfather returned the hug.

"What's this?" he asked.

"Oh, Grandfather, we missed you!" Benny answered.

His eyes twinkled. "Perhaps I should go out more often," he said.

"We didn't know where you were,"

Henry said. He tried to keep the concern from his voice, but it seeped through.

Grandfather grew serious. "I'm sorry if I worried you. I decided to take a walk this morning."

Jessie looked at Henry. *Did the telephone call cause Grandfather to go out early this morning?* she wondered. The look in Henry's eye told her he was asking himself the same question.

Benny put his hands on his hips. "You should have told us, Grandfather," he said.

Mr. Alden smiled and took Benny in his arms.

Jessie said, "Let's have breakfast."

Benny ran over to the table. "I forgot all about eating."

"We can't let that happen," Grandfather teased.

Each poured cereal from the boxes Jessie had put on the table. They topped their choices with sliced bananas and strawberries.

"I have good news," Grandfather said. "I can be your guide today. Is there anything special you'd like to see?"

They named some of the places they wanted to see. The Museum of Science and Industry was the first on everybody's list.

"There's a real submarine there," Benny said. "And a great big model train."

Grandfather nodded. "There's so much to see and do, we could spend an entire day there."

Violet held up a leaflet. "I'd like to see the Shedd Aquarium," she said.

Henry was interested in the Field Museum of Natural History. "I'd like to see the dinosaur skeletons," he said.

"Me, too," Benny agreed.

"We'll be here a few more days," Grandfather said. "We can probably see it all." He thumbed through the pile of Chicago information.

Clue #3 was among those papers. Grandfather would surely find it. The Aldens held their breaths, wondering how they would explain it without telling him about the mystery.

Mr. Alden put the folded clue aside without looking at it. The children relaxed.

"You decide. I'm going to take a shower and change my clothes."

Henry and Benny cleared away the rest of the breakfast things and did the dishes.

Jessie unfolded the latest clue. She studied the cow and the lantern and the burned city. It all fit together except for the modern fire engine. What did it mean? "Unless we visit the place where the fire started," she said, "we'll never solve this clue."

Violet opened Grandfather's workbook to reread the section on the fire. "Cow or not, the fire started somewhere in or near Mrs. O'Leary's barn."

Henry came in from the kitchen. "Then we have to find her barn."

At his heels, Benny said, "Didn't it burn up?"

"The barn's gone," Henry said, "but there might be something on the spot where it stood — a plaque or museum or something. Seeing it might help us figure out this clue."

Jessie looked at a map. "The barn was on De Koven Street." She ran her finger along the map. "Here it is." She showed the others.

Henry put the clue in his back pocket. "That's it, then, we have to go to De Koven Street."

"Good choice," Grandfather said as he came into the living room.

"Is there a museum or something there, Grandfather?" Violet asked.

Grandfather shrugged. "Truth is, I've never been there. Never had the time. But I've always thought it would be interesting to see where the fire started."

Benny grabbed his Cubs cap and off they went.

Willard was outside. "Your car awaits." He pointed to a car at the curb and handed Mr. Alden the keys.

The children were puzzled. How did Willard know they would need a car?

Grandfather seemed to know what they were thinking. As he pulled into traffic, he said, "We could have taken public transportation, but Cob thought we might like to drive today."

Henry studied a map. "Do you know how to find De Koven Street, Grandfather? It's only a block long."

Mr. Alden nodded. "Cob gave me directions," he said.

Henry, Jessie, and Violet thought nothing of that remark until Benny asked, "How did Mr. Piper know where we were going?" It was a good question. How could Mr. Piper know where they were going when they had just decided this morning? They waited expectantly for the answer.

It never came.

Instead, Grandfather directed their attention to the sights along the way. Before long, he pulled up to a glazed red brick building. High on one corner, white letters spelled out CHICAGO FIRE ACADEMY. Near the entrance was a giant gold sculpture of flames.

"Is this a school for firemen?" Benny asked.

Violet asked, "Is this where the Great Chicago Fire started?"

"Let's go inside and see," Grandfather answered.

An old red hose wagon was displayed in the lobby. Firefighters in small groups at the information desk and in the hall beyond smiled at them as they entered. One of them stepped forward. "Welcome," he said. "Can I help you?"

They asked him about Mrs. O'Leary.

He led them to a plaque on the wall. A chain connected to two brass fire nozzles set it apart from other displays.

Henry read the inscription. "On this site stood the home and barn of Mrs. O'Leary, where the Chicago fire of 1871 started. Although there are many versions of the story of its origin, the real cause of the fire has never been determined."

"The barn was right here," the firefighter said. "The gold flame outside stands where her house was."

Jessie was impressed. "And now, on the same spot, people are trained to fight fires."

They wandered down the hall looking at the glass-covered wall displays of historical photos and drawings.

Outside, Benny's eyes grew wide. Shiny

fire trucks of all kinds filled the yard. One of the firemen helped Benny and Violet climb inside.

Henry pulled Jessie aside. "This is the place," he said. He dug the clue out of his pocket. They both looked at it. There could be no doubt. Here, just as in the picture, the past and the present stood side by side.

"Do you suppose the next clue is here?" Jessie asked.

"Keep your eyes open," Henry answered.

Benny skipped over to them. "Did you see me in that fire engine?" he asked excitedly. "I'm going to be a firefighter when I grow up!"

There was so much to see and do, they spent another hour touring the site. But they did not find the next clue.

Back at the car, Grandfather said, "It's early yet. How about visiting one of those places we talked about this morning?"

The Alden children all spoke at once, each naming a favored place.

Grandfather laughed. "I'll choose." He

opened the car door and everyone got in.

They cruised along the lake past a busy harbor and through a beautiful green park.

"Who has a map?" Benny asked.

Jessie pulled one out of her backpack.

"Why do you want a map, Benny?" Henry wanted to know.

"To see where we're going," Benny said. After a long silence, he said, "I figured it out!" Before he could say another word, Mr. Alden pulled into a big parking lot. "There it is!" Benny pointed straight ahead. "The Museum of Science and Industry!"

They scooted out of the car and hurried across the parking lot. They dashed up the broad cement stairway, past huge round columns, through tall doors, into the vast building.

They had so much fun they forgot about the mystery.

But not for long!

CHAPTER 8

The Final Clue

Grandfather pulled up in front of their apartment building. Willard was outside, talking to a man in a long raincoat and a broad-brimmed hat. Something striped was sticking out of his coat pocket.

Willard waved and came to the curb. The other man hurried inside.

Henry was the only one who noticed.

Willard opened the car doors. "Welcome back," he said.

"Does that man live here?" Henry asked.

Willard looked around. "What man?"

"The man you were talking to."

Willard laughed. "I talk to everybody!"

Grandfather came around from the driver's side. "Will you see that this car gets back where it belongs?"

Willard took the keys Mr. Alden held out to him. "Be happy to oblige," he said.

They met Chad inside. "I was looking for you," he told them. "I wanted to talk to you about tomorrow — where you want to go."

"We can talk about it now," Jessie said.

Chad shook his head. "Sorry. I can't. I have an appointment." He stepped back toward the doors. "You talk it over. I'll see you in the morning."

They headed toward the elevators.

Grandfather stopped suddenly. "Why don't you go on upstairs," he said. "I want to get a newspaper."

"Do you have the key, Henry?" Violet asked.

Henry patted his shirt pocket. "I remembered it today."

"Go along, then," Grandfather said. "I'll be up shortly."

While they were waiting for the elevator, Benny said, "It sure seems like Grandfather is reading a lot of newspapers."

"You're right, Benny," said Jessie. "He just bought one this morning."

On the way up to the twentieth floor, they talked about the museum.

"Of all the things we saw, I liked the model train best," Benny said. "It reminded me of our boxcar."

The elevator doors snapped open.

As they approached 2004, Jessie saw something. One by one, the other Aldens saw it, too. Someone had put an envelope under their door. Part of it stuck out into the hall.

Jessie picked it up. "This must be the fourth clue," she said.

Benny sighed. "We haven't even solved the third one!"

"Yes, we have, Benny," Violet said. "It was the Fire Academy." She looked at Henry and Jessie. "Right?"

Henry nodded. "Had to be," he said. He opened the door and they all went inside.

Jessie slipped off her backpack and set it on a chair. Then, she examined the envelope.

"Open it, Jessie," Violet urged.

Jessie opened the envelope. "It's another collage," she said.

Benny stood up and leaned across the table. "Of what?"

Jessie laid the paper on the table where they could all see.

"It's more like a map," Henry said.

Violet turned the paper toward her. "It's a map *and* a collage!"

She was right. The crudely drawn map was topped with cut-out pictures of all the places they had been. The Water Tower was at the top and the Museum of Science and Industry was at the bottom. In between were the Michigan Avenue Bridge, the Art Institute, Grant Park, the Fire Academy — even their apartment building and the pizza place!

"How can this be a clue?" Henry wondered aloud. He held the map up.

"There's writing on the back, Henry," Benny told him.

Henry turned the paper over. "Here we go," he said. "This says, 'The Final Clue.' " He continued reading:

Buried deep
Beneath the rest
Is the treasure
I think best.
Can you find
A place like home
Resting on
A bed of stone?

Henry stopped reading. No one said a word. He reread the clue to himself. Once, twice, three times. Finally he looked up. "Any ideas?" he asked the others.

They stared at him with wide eyes. No one knew what the clue meant.

"Who is doing this?" Jessie's tone was full of frustration.

"Chad was here when we got back," Violet reminded them. "He could have slipped the clue under the door."

"But he has a key," Henry said.

"I think Willard did it," Benny piped up.

"Willard could have brought the envelope up here," Henry said.

"And he could have made the map and written the clue, too."

"Let's go back over what we know." Jessie took the first two clues out of her backpack.

Henry removed the third clue from his back pocket and set it and the final clue beside the others. "Go back to the first day," he said.

"Willard gave us the clue about the Water Tower," Benny said.

Violet nodded. "We were waiting for Chad in the lobby."

"And Chad talked to Willard outside," Jessie added. "Then Willard gave us the envelope."

"Don't forget that other man," Henry said. "He was talking to Willard, too."

The others hadn't thought about the strange man. No one had ever suggested he had anything to do with this mystery.

Thinking about the man always made Benny giggle. "The man with the big mustache," he said. "How did it get so crooked?"

"It wasn't crooked the first time we saw him," Jessie said.

"That was later, Benny — at the ball game," Violet reminded him. "Maybe he made a mistake trying to trim it."

"Did anyone notice that man with Willard today?" Henry asked.

"The man in the raincoat?" Jessie said.

Henry nodded. "Did anyone see his face?"

No one had.

"I thought he might be the man with the mustache," Henry continued. "When we pulled up, he hurried away. It was as if he didn't want us to see him."

None of the others had noticed that.

"He had something sticking out of his pocket," Henry said. "It looked like a striped cap."

"The man at the ballpark wore a striped cap," Violet remembered.

"And the man we saw talking to Willard that morning was carrying one," Jessie added.

"Like a railroad engineer's hat," Violet said.

"So the man downstairs today could be the same man," Henry concluded.

"Let's say he gave Willard the first clue." Jessie held up the second clue. "But what about this one? I found it in my backpack after we had been to the Water Tower. We didn't see him there."

Benny frowned in thought. "Maybe he put the clue there before we got there. Or Willard — he went there early in the morning and hid the envelope."

"I looked all around that building," Henry said. "Inside and out."

"Then I dropped the leaflets," Jessie said. "We already decided I must have picked up the clue then."

"I picked up most of the leaflets," Benny said. "And I didn't see an envelope."

"And Grandfather picked up the others," Violet said. "The envelope must have been with those."

"The person who dropped that envelope knew we'd find it," Henry said. "Whoever did it had to be right there with us."

Henry smiled triumphantly. "There were only two people who could have done that: Chad or Grandfather."

Benny stood up. "Chad did it," he said. "Now can we eat?"

"Not until Grandfather comes back," Jessie said.

Suddenly they realized that Mr. Alden had been downstairs a long time — much longer than it would take to buy a newspaper.

"He always takes a long time," Benny said. "He's probably talking to Willard."

But the others weren't so sure. They remembered last night's telephone call, and Grandfather's long walk that morning. None of the Aldens could remember seeing Grandfather reading the first newspaper he'd bought.

"Let's go look for him!" Henry said.

Before he could finish the thought, Jessie was out the door, Violet at her heels.

Henry sprinted after them, saying, "Come on, Benny!"

CHAPTER 9

Another Phone Call

The elevator seemed to take forever. None of the Aldens spoke. They were wondering what they would find when they reached the ground floor. Grandfather had been strange during this trip. How did he know they would be at the Water Tower that day? He said Chad told him. No one remembered that — not even Chad. And later, at the ball game, he disappeared. He told them he stopped to buy Benny a cap, but that wasn't true. Henry was with him when he bought it. Then there was the phone call in the night. And all the trips to get newspapers! Added together, these events got the Alden children thinking.

"Maybe he decided to read the paper down in the lobby," Jessie suggested.

That was a possibility. Comfortable chairs and couches lined the inner lobby. He could read the paper *and* chat with Willard.

The doors slid open. The children hurried out. They glanced around. No one was sitting on the chairs or couches.

The Aldens looked beyond to the outer lobby. Then they saw Grandfather. Off in a corner, he was talking to someone — a man who carried a raincoat and a broad-brimmed hat.

"There he is!" Benny said, darting ahead.

Henry caught him. "Wait, Benny," he said. "Let's see what we can find out." He put a finger to his lips, a signal for his sisters and brother to be quiet.

They crept to the wall between the two rooms and pressed themselves against it. One of the doors was propped open. Still, it was difficult to hear Grandfather's words over the voices of the other people in the outer lobby. They did hear the tone; it sounded as if the two men were having a disagreement.

Henry motioned for the others to follow. He went through the doors. Then he stopped short. "Why, Grandfather!" he said, pretending to be surprised. "We were just looking for you."

Mr. Alden's face turned red and his eyes opened wide. He was genuinely surprised. He opened his mouth to speak, but nothing came out.

The other man stepped forward. He held out his hand. "I'm Jacob Piper," he said. "You must be the very special grandchildren I've heard so much about."

The children shook his hand. They all said, "It's nice to meet you."

Something about the man seemed familiar.

Henry glanced at the raincoat and hat Mr. Piper carried. "Didn't we see you here earlier?" he asked. "Talking to Willard?"

Mr. Piper looked at Mr. Alden, then back

at the children. He didn't respond. Instead, he said, "I want to take you out to dinner. I've been trying to persuade your grandfather."

Mr. Alden recovered his voice. "I told Cob you were probably too tired. After all, you've had a busy day."

Relief flooded the younger Aldens. So that's what the two men had been talking about.

"I'm never too tired to eat," Benny piped up.

Everyone laughed.

"So you'll come?" Mr. Piper said. He sounded pleased.

"We'll have to clean up and change," Mr. Alden said.

Mr. Piper turned to Benny. "Can you wait that long?"

"I think so." Benny sounded very serious — and uncertain.

Mr. Piper laughed. "Good," he said. "Meet you in an hour." He put on his hat and turned to leave. "Remember: X marks the spot," he said as he went out the door.

That seemed a strange thing to say.

"X marks what spot?" Benny asked.

"We'll find out," Mr. Alden said. "Cob is fond of riddles."

The younger Aldens were ready before their grandfather.

In the living room, Henry said, "Mr. Piper is the man we saw earlier — the man in the raincoat."

Jessie nodded. "I thought so, too, Henry. But when you asked him, he didn't answer."

"Didn't you say there was something striped sticking out of his pocket, Henry?" Violet asked.

"Yes. A railroad cap — the kind the man with the mustache wore."

"I didn't see anything like that," Benny said.

"Mr. Piper was carrying the raincoat," Henry responded. "It was all folded over. You couldn't see his pockets." He sighed. "But I was on the wrong track. He's not the man with the mustache."

Jessie sat down at the table. "Let's look over the clues again," she said.

They listed what they knew. The first clue had been given to them by Willard. The second was picked up outside the Water Tower. The third was at the Art Institute on the student bulletin board. Chad gave them that one. The fourth and final clue had been slipped under their door. Knowing where they had gotten the clues did not tell them who had written them.

"We know one thing for sure," Henry concluded. "Chad was with us — or nearby — every time."

It did seem likely that Chad was behind the mystery. But even though they had watched him for telltale signs of guilt, there had been none. He had certainly acted surprised to find the envelope on the student bulletin board. He had even suggested someone might be following them.

That thought prompted Violet to say, "Remember that man at the Art Institute? We thought he might be the man with the mustache."

"But he wasn't," Benny said. "He didn't have a mustache. Just bushy eyebrows."

"The two men did look alike," Henry said. "Both were balding and both were about the same size."

Jessie nodded. "We thought they might be brothers."

Grandfather came into the room. "Are we ready?" he asked.

Benny's stomach growled. Everyone heard it.

Mr. Alden laughed. "I think that's a *yes!*"

Because it was a warm, clear evening, they decided to walk.

Thinking about the mystery, Henry asked, "Grandfather, have you known Mr. Piper for a long time?"

"For many years. I knew his father, too. And I watched Chad grow up."

"Has he always been in the paper business?" Jessie asked.

Grandfather nodded. "And his father before him. Somewhere along the line, the family was connected with railroading. At one time, Chicago was the railroad center of the country."

That pleased Benny. "Maybe I could ask

Mr. Piper how I can get to be a railroad engineer."

Mr. Alden chuckled. "I'm sure he could help," he said. Grandfather stopped before a glass and steel building. "We're here."

The Alden children stepped back to look up. They couldn't believe their eyes. Starting at the broad base and climbing to the narrower top were a series of gigantic steel X's.

"X marks the spot," the younger Aldens all said at once.

Grandfather laughed. "Right you are," he said. "Another mystery solved!" He told them the name of the building: the John Hancock. "The X's are not decoration; they're essential to the structure," he added as he glanced upward. "This was the tallest building in Chicago until the Sears Tower was built."

They hurried inside to an elevator. It ascended so quickly their ears popped. The first stop was a restaurant on the ninety-fifth floor, where Jacob Piper was waiting.

He led them to a table by the windows.

Behind him, Henry and Jessie noticed something they hadn't seen before: Mr. Piper's dark hair framed a bald spot.

"Here we are," Mr. Piper said.

Outside the windows, the lake and city stretched as far as the eye could see.

Beside them, Mr. Piper murmured, "No matter how many times I see this sight, it still thrills me."

"And no wonder," Grandfather said. "It's spectacular."

They sat down and opened their menus.

Benny read the selections. Everything looked good. He glanced at the prices. Everything was very expensive. He closed his menu. "Maybe I'm not so hungry after all."

Mr. Piper seemed to read his mind. "This is my treat," he said. "I come here on special occasions only. Meeting you finally, and our being together — that's reason to celebrate."

After that, they all relaxed.

Mr. Piper was easy to talk to. He told them about the paper business and about his family. "I hoped Chad could join us tonight," he said, "but with work and school, he hasn't much spare time."

"Chad's a very good artist," Violet said. "And a very good teacher."

Mr. Piper smiled. "He told me you were good, too, Violet."

When their dinners arrived, Jessie said, "This looks beautiful — almost too good to eat."

Benny picked up his fork. "No food looks *that* good," he said.

Throughout the meal, Henry was distracted. Mr. Piper's upper lip and lower forehead were red, and he kept scratching them.

Benny noticed it, too, and while they were waiting for dessert, he asked, "What's that red stuff on your face, Mr. Piper?"

"Benny!" Jessie scolded.

"That's all right, Jessie," Mr. Piper said. "It does look strange. People have been asking me about it all week. It's some kind of rash."

"You must be allergic to something, Cob," Mr. Alden said.

Mr. Piper smiled. "I wonder what it could be."

Back at the apartment, the children went straight to bed. Grandfather sat down to read his newspaper.

The phone rang.

This time, all four Aldens heard it. Behind their doors, they listened carefully.

"I told you that before," Grandfather said. "You just have to be patient." And, "No, I won't do that. Not yet." There was a pause, then, "Trust me. It won't be long."

"Let's go talk to the girls," Benny whispered.

Henry shook his head. "Not now, Benny. Grandfather will hear us."

Across the hall, Violet and Jessie had a similar conversation.

For now, there was nothing they could do.

X Marks the Spot

Grandfather knocked on their doors. "Wake up, sleepyheads!" he called. "It's another beautiful day in Chicago!"

For a few brief seconds, the younger Aldens forgot their concern. But when they were fully awake, the memory of last night's telephone call resurfaced.

"Grandfather sounds cheerful," Violet said. She was hoping they had been wrong. Perhaps the two late-night phone conversations did not mean trouble after all.

Jessie slipped into her slacks. "He does,"

she agreed. But still she was fearful. Grandfather had a way of putting a good face on things. If he *was* in some kind of trouble, he would not want to worry them.

They went out into the hall. The boys' door opened and Henry and Benny came out.

"Grandfather certainly sounds cheerful," Henry said.

"He's pretending," Benny whispered.

The table was set with juice and fresh fruit and a big platter of sweet rolls.

"Well, there you are!" Grandfather said as they sat down. "I was up early," he said. "I went to the bakery." He held up a piece of paper. "But I remembered to leave a note in case you woke up and found me gone."

Jessie and Henry looked at each other. They had left the clues spread out on this table. Their maps and leaflets were stacked at one end. Were the clues there? Had Grandfather seen them? If he had, wouldn't he ask about them? How would they answer his questions?

Grandfather saw Jessie staring at the

stack. "I piled those things together," he said.

Surely he hadn't noticed the clues.

"I'll be busy all day today. What do you and Chad have planned?"

"We haven't talked to him," Henry said.

"He was here yesterday," Benny put in, "just before we found —"

Jessie was quick to interrupt. "He was here when we got back from the museum," she said, "but he didn't have time to talk."

Grandfather nodded. "That's right."

Violet said, "I'm hoping we can do some more sketching."

"It's a fine day for it." Mr. Alden pushed his chair away from the table. "I guess I'd better get a move on." He went into his bedroom.

Violet leaned close to the others. "Should we ask him about the phone calls?"

"There's probably nothing to tell us," Henry said. "He seems fine."

Mr. Alden came in carrying a briefcase. "Can you find enough to do until Chad gets here?" he asked.

They all said, "Yes. Plenty!"

As soon as he was gone, Jessie dug through the pile of brochures. "Funny Grandfather didn't see the clues," she said as she spread them out.

Violet looked at them and sighed. "Where do we start?"

"Let's not think about the writer of the clues," Henry said.

Benny tapped the final clue. "We should solve this."

Jessie turned the map over. She read the first four lines of the verse. " 'Buried deep/ Beneath the rest,' " she repeated.

"We might need a shovel for this one," Henry joked.

"Read the rest, Jessie," Benny said.

" 'Can you find/ A place like home . . .' "

"What does that mean?" Violet asked.

"*Home* could be Grandfather's house," Jessie said.

"Or our boxcar," added Violet. "After all, that was our home once."

Henry said, "The last part says, 'Resting on/ A bed of stone.' "

Jessie frowned. "This is the hardest clue yet."

Henry turned the paper over. "We've been to all the places pictured on this map."

"Could that mean this clue leads to someplace we've already been?" Jessie said.

The telephone rang. Jessie answered. It was Chad.

"Something's come up," he said. "I'm sorry, but I can't get there this morning."

"Oh, that's all right, Chad."

"I may be able to get away this afternoon," Chad went on. "If not, I'll see you tonight."

"Tonight?"

"At dinner with my father."

Jessie was confused. "But we had dinner with him last night."

After a brief silence, Chad said, "I . . . uh . . . maybe I misunderstood." He told her he would phone later and hung up.

Jessie repeated his message.

They had mixed feelings about it: On the one hand, they were sorry to miss a morning of sightseeing; on the other, they were happy to have time to work on the clue.

"Chad didn't seem to know we were with his father last night," Jessie said.

Violet was puzzled. "But he must have been invited. Mr. Piper said Chad was too busy to be there."

"Maybe Chad forgot," Benny suggested.

"Or got the dates mixed up," Henry added.

They returned their attention to the clue. But it was no use. They could not solve this part of the puzzle.

Henry turned the map this way and that, moving it close to his eyes and far away. "Look here," he said at last. He pointed to several pictures: the Water Tower, the Art Institute, the Fire Academy.

A small X was penciled on each one.

"Those are the places the clues sent us to," Violet observed.

"X marks the spot," Henry said.

Benny jumped in his chair. "Mr. Piper said that!"

"Mr. Piper can't be behind this," Jessie said. "When would he have the time? He's been at all those meetings with Grandfather." She leaned toward the map. "Are there any other X's?"

They took turns looking. On the first try, no one could find a single additional mark. Second time around, Violet saw something.

"This looks like an X." She pointed it out to the others.

"You found it, Violet!" Benny said.

Henry's mouth dropped open. "And it's on the picture of the building we're in!"

They were stunned to silence. Could this mean the final clue led right here? But where could the treasure be?

"Let's go talk to Willard," Jessie suggested. "Maybe he knows something about this building that would help."

Willard smiled as the Aldens approached. "On your way out?"

"We've been wondering about this building," Jessie told him.

"Wonderful old place, isn't it?" the man said. "Solid as a rock. They don't build 'em like this anymore."

"Are there things about it people don't know?" Violet asked.

"Ahhh, this grand old place keeps its secrets." Willard's eyes twinkled.

"What secrets?" Benny asked.

"If I told you, they wouldn't be secrets, would they, now?"

"You could tell us," Benny said. "We won't tell anyone."

Willard threw his head back and laughed. "I've been sworn to secrecy. I'm sorry," he said.

Just then several people came in. Willard went to greet them.

The Aldens looked around the lobby. Was there anything here that might help in their search? Henry noticed two doors. Painted the same color as the walls, they were barely visible.

"Wait here," he whispered. Hoping Willard wouldn't notice, he slipped across the lobby. He tried one door and then the other. Both were locked.

CHAPTER 11

Buried Treasure

Disappointed, the Aldens went back upstairs.

Just inside the apartment door, Violet picked up something. "What's this?" She held it in her open hand. It was fuzzy and black.

"It looks like some strange caterpillar," Jessie said.

Benny took it between two fingers. He held it under his nose. "Do I look like the man with the mustache?"

Jessie laughed, then grew serious. "Let me

see that." She turned it over. "The back is covered with something — dried paste or glue."

All at once, the four Aldens came to the same conclusion: "It's part of a disguise!"

"The man in the overalls wore it!" Jessie said.

"That would explain why the mustache was crooked. The glue was dry, so it no longer stuck as well," Henry said.

Violet took the object from Henry. "But it isn't big enough to be a mustache. It's more like" — she put it above her eye — "an eyebrow!"

Jessie sank to a chair. "Do you suppose . . ."

"Yes! That's it!" Henry said. "The man with the mustache and the one with the bushy eyebrows — they're one person!"

"The *same* person!" Violet said.

"*What* person?" Benny asked.

"Whoever was up here while we were talking to Willard," Henry said. "Whoever dropped the eyebrow — *that* person!"

"Chad has a key," Jessie reminded them.

"We would have seen him come into the building," Violet said.

"Unless there's another way in," Henry added.

"Maybe he hid somewhere in the hall until we went out," Benny suggested.

Jessie's mind took her in another direction. "Chad was never with us when we saw that strange man," she said. "But he was always nearby."

Slowly, the others understood her meaning. Chad could be the man in the disguise!

"But he never wore overalls," Henry said.

"Maybe he carried them in his knapsack," Benny said.

"Where would he have changed into them?" Henry persisted.

They were getting nowhere. Every question about the man led to several new questions. Finally they sat down with the clues and began listing everything they knew.

Violet puzzled over the lines "Buried deep/Beneath the rest."

"The X is marked on this building. Do

you think there could be something underneath it?" she asked at last.

Henry thought about that. Then he remembered: "Chad told us Chicago has a lower level."

"With train tracks and everything," Benny added.

"Maybe it runs under this building," Jessie said.

Benny sprang out of his chair and headed for the door. "Let's go find out!"

Downstairs, Grandfather Alden huddled with someone wearing bib overalls — a man with a mustache and one bushy eyebrow! Talking intently, the two stepped out of sight. By the time the Alden children reached the outer lobby, the men were gone.

"They didn't go out the front door," Violet said. "We would've seen them."

Henry was baffled. "But they couldn't just . . . disappear!"

"Look, Henry!" Jessie pointed to the doors Henry had tried earlier. One of them was open.

"Let's ask Willard where it leads," Violet suggested.

But Willard was busy outside.

And Benny was already across the room. His brother and sisters followed. They slipped through the door and came upon a stairwell. They heard voices below, and then . . . nothing.

Taking the lead, Henry crept down the stairs. The others stayed close behind him.

At the bottom of the stairs was another door. Slowly, cautiously, Henry cracked it open and peeked into the dimness beyond.

Henry let out a soft whistle. Then he said, "Wow!"

"What is it, Henry?" Jessie murmured.

Henry opened the door. There in the murky light was a lone railroad coach!

Stunned, they moved outside to the walkway. They wondered where the car had come from and why it was there.

After a long silence, Violet said, " 'A place like home'! The clue was about our home in the boxcar!"

" 'Resting on/A bed of stone,' " Jessie quoted.

"Gravel, or stone, is used to make railroad ties stable," Henry said.

"We've solved the final clue!" Violet said.

But the mystery was yet to be fully explained. They still had no idea who was behind this strange treasure hunt — or the reason for it.

Henry motioned them to stay where they were. He sneaked up onto the observation platform and peered through a window.

"What do you see?" Violet asked.

Suddenly a voice behind her said, "I see you've found the treasure I think best."

Jessie, Violet, and Benny spun around. Their mouths dropped open in surprise. "You!"

Jacob Piper pulled off a fake mustache and one bushy eyebrow.

Just then, Grandfather appeared on the platform beside Henry. "I told you, Cob," he said. "My grandchildren are smart. I knew they'd figure out our little game."

Jacob Piper and Grandfather! Together,

they were responsible for this baffling mystery!

Mr. Piper climbed onto the platform. "Come on aboard."

Astonished, the children followed him.

Cob swept his arm in a circle. "Welcome to my home."

Benny stared at him. "You *live* here?"

Cob laughed. "It's very comfortable," he said. He proudly showed them everything: a desk that opened into a large table; chairs that turned into beds; a stainless steel kitchen, where something bubbled on the compact stove.

"That smells good," Benny said.

"Spaghetti sauce for our supper," Cob told him.

Questions swirled through the Aldens' minds, but they were too amazed to ask them. Still, the two men provided answers.

Grandfather said, "When I told Cob you like mysteries, he planned this treasure hunt."

"It was a good way for you to see my favorite city," Mr. Piper told them. "But I was afraid you wouldn't solve it. I wanted to tell

you. Your grandfather and I argued about it."

That explained the telephone calls.

"I was worried about the whole thing," Mr. Alden continued. "I didn't know how I was going to give you the clue at the Water Tower. Fortunately, Jessie, you dropped the maps. I slipped the envelope in with them."

"And I just missed seeing Chad at the Art Institute," Mr. Piper said.

Henry found his voice. "So Chad didn't know."

Mr. Piper shook his head. "I was afraid he'd give it away."

"How about Willard?" Benny asked.

"He knew something was going on, but he never figured it out." Cob held up the mustache. "I'm not very good at this disguise business."

Benny snickered. "I never saw a crooked mustache before."

"I didn't know it was crooked!" Cob laughed.

Now Henry knew what caused Cob's rash. "You're allergic to the glue."

Cob nodded. "And I couldn't make it stick. Today I lost an eyebrow."

"We found it in the apartment," Violet told him.

Cobb nodded. "I thought I might find something in the apartment to tell me how close you were to finding this car."

"Not very close," Jessie said.

"Oh, you're good detectives," Grandfather said. "You would have figured it out."

Now that all the puzzle pieces were in place, Cob gave them a new challenge. "See if you can set the table for eight." He turned to Mr. Alden. "James, you and I will cook."

Benny counted. There were six of them. "Who else is coming?"

"Chad and Willard," Cob answered. "They didn't know it, but they played important parts in our little game."

It was tight, but they all fit. During dinner, the Aldens told Chad and Willard about the mystery and how they had solved it.

"I knew you were looking for something," Willard said.

Chad just kept shaking his head. "Dad, you planned all this?"

"And more," Mr. Piper said. "I've saved the best part for last."

Benny jumped in his chair. "Tell us! Please!"

"This is my own private train car," he began. "It belonged to my grandfather. He was in the railroad business. After he retired, he brought it to his backyard."

"We have a boxcar in our backyard," Violet said.

Mr. Piper nodded. "So James told me. And just like you, I played in it every chance I got."

Benny looked around. "This is much fancier than our boxcar."

"It didn't always look like it does today," Cob said. "Time and weather had done their work. Then one day I decided to restore it."

"By yourself?" Jessie asked.

"Yes," Cob answered. "It took a long

time. After I had finished it, I thought, why not live in it? It's been here ever since. It's my hobby — the only way I relax from the paper business. I rent the track. I travel in it, too. That's my final surprise: I have a trip planned for next week."

The Alden children's minds raced ahead of him. They exchanged excited glances.

Cob laughed. "You are quick," he said. "I can tell you've guessed it. After you've seen the rest of the city, we'll hook this car to an eastbound train and take you home to Greenfield!"

The Aldens laughed with delight.

Willard laughed, too. "I'd say you Aldens found what you were looking for!"

"Much more!" Violet said.

Mr. Piper raised his glass. "A toast to buried treasure."

Henry looked around the table at his sisters and brother, Grandfather, the Pipers, and Willard. These people were his family and friends. They were the real treasures. He raised his glass. "And to those in plain sight," he said.

Gertrude Chandler Warner discovered when she was teaching that many readers who like an exciting story could find no books that were both easy and fun to read. She decided to try to meet this need, and her first book, *The Boxcar Children*, quickly proved she had succeeded.

Miss Warner drew on her own experiences to write the mystery. As a child she spent hours watching trains go by on the tracks opposite her family home. She often dreamed about what it would be like to set up housekeeping in a caboose or freight car — the situation the Alden children find themselves in.

When Miss Warner received requests for more adventures involving Henry, Jessie, Violet, and Benny Alden, she began additional stories. In each, she chose a special setting and introduced unusual or eccentric characters who liked the unpredictable.

While the mystery element is central to each of Miss Warner's books, she never thought of them as strictly juvenile mysteries. She liked to stress the Aldens' independence and resourcefulness and their solid New England devotion to using up and making do. The Aldens go about most of their adventures with as little adult supervision as possible — something else that delights young readers.

Miss Warner lived in Putnam, Connecticut, until her death in 1979. During her lifetime, she received hundreds of letters from girls and boys telling her how much they liked her books.